A Day With Babe

written by Susan Kassirer
illustrated by Jan Gerardi

inchworm PRESS ™

UNIVERSAL

"Cock-a-doodle doo!" The rooster crowed, and it was time to get up at Hoggett farm.

Babe turned over in his bed of straw. Then he yawned. Babe loved his job as the only sheep pig in the whole world, but just like all the other animals, he was happy for a day off. And today was that day. The Hoggetts were going to town.

Babe wasn't quite sure what to do on his day off. So he asked his mom, Fly, the sheepdog who had raised him.

"I plan to sleep late and get up when I'm good and ready," said Fly with a yawn.

Babe knew that Fly was very wise, so he decided to do just what she did. He turned over and closed his eyes.

But soon Babe heard Mrs. Hoggett rustling around in her kitchen getting breakfast, and before he knew it his tummy was growling.

"Oh, well," he thought. "I may as well get up and eat. Then I'll come back to the barn and take a nice long nap!"

So Babe tiptoed quietly out of the barn.

Meanwhile, Duchess the cat had her own ideas about what to do on her day off. Duchess's job was to stay indoors, purr, and sit around looking pretty for her boss, Mrs. Hoggett. She couldn't wait to sneak outdoors just to make sure that none of the other animals had nicer homes, fancier food, or better toys.

Babe ate a good hearty breakfast. Then he headed back to the barn, as planned. But as he walked along Babe heard a long cry coming from above. Babe looked up. There was Duchess, stuck high in an oak tree.

"Babe, get me down!" cried the frightened cat.

Ever since Babe had arrived at Hoggett farm, Duchess had been nothing but trouble for him. But Babe knew he couldn't turn his back on her. He thought and thought, and finally came up with an idea.

"Just hold on there, Duchess," he said. "I'll be right back."

Quickly, Babe ran to the sheep field. He knew it was asking quite a lot of the sheep to work on their day off, but maybe if he asked very nicely. . .

"Well, hello there, sheep," Babe said. "Didn't think you'd be seeing me today, did you?" He gave a friendly little laugh. "But you know that cat, the one that belongs to the boss's wife? Well, it seems she is in some trouble."

"What is it, Babe?" said one of the sheep. "You know we'll always help you out."

"How kind of you!" said Babe. "You're all so good at standing in nice straight lines. Have you ever thought of, er, standing one on top of the other?"

The sheep followed Babe to the tree and obediently carried out his instructions, just as they did on regular working days.

"Here, now. I think making a ladder is the best idea," said Babe. "That's right, three on the bottom, then two. My goodness, you are all so good at this. Thank you very much."

Within minutes Duchess was climbing down the finest sheep ladder ever made.

"Whew, now I'm really ready for that nap," thought Babe once Duchess was safely back indoors. Again he headed for the barn. But it was much too hot in there, and he knew he couldn't stay.

"It's noon. That's why it's so hot in there," said Ferdinand the duck, pointing up at the sun. "The best thing to do at noon it to have lunch and take a nap by the pond."

"Thank you, Ferdy," said Babe. "What a good idea!"

After eating the tasty lunch that the Hoggetts had left out for him, Babe headed for the pond.

Unfortunately, the ducks had gotten there first and had decided to have a noisy water party!

Babe accepted their invitation to stay, and politely chatted with them for awhile. But it was much too noisy to nap, so after some time Babe excused himself and headed on his way.

Babe decided to go to his favorite spot by the brook. But it certainly seemed that luck was against the little sheep pig today. No sooner did he lay down in the soft grass than the sky began to fill with clouds. Within moments buckets of rain came pouring down.

As Babe took shelter under some bushes he heard a familiar noise.

"Wa-a-h," bleated a little sheep. Babe followed the sad sound.

"Am I glad to see you, Babe," said a frightened ewe. "I thought I'd take a walk on my own for my day off. I get tired of following the other sheep all the time. I had fun, but now I'm lost!"

"That's okay," said Babe. "I'll get you back home. Follow me!"

And so Babe did what he did best . . . he led the ewe right to her flock.

By the time Babe got back to the farm, the Hoggetts had returned and Mrs. Hoggett was putting out Babe's dinner.

As Babe ate he realized that his day off had come and gone. And he had never taken his nap.

Fly had slept late, Duchess had escaped from the house, the ducks had a party, and the ewe had taken a walk on her own. But what had Babe done?

That's exactly what the cow asked the little sheep pig as the animals all settled down for the night.

"Well," said Babe. "I thought I'd sleep late, like Fly. But I was hungry, so I got up. Then I wanted to take a nap, but it was too hot in the barn, and too noisy at the pond . . . ."

"So didn't you do anything on your day off?" asked the cow.

"Well, yes," said Babe, "I rescued Duchess from a tree, I came across a water party on the pond, I ran for shelter from the rain, I showed a lost sheep the way home . . ."

"My goodness, you did do a lot!" said Fly, as all the other animals nodded. "You had a day of adventure!"

"Hmmm, I guess I did," said Babe. "That must be it. I had a day of adventure!"

Overhead the stars twinkled and the moon glowed, and from the pond rose a chorus of spring peepers and frogs. The barn was quiet and cool, and Babe had a full tummy and a roof over his head. As he lay very still he thought of the fun and exciting things he had done during the day.

Then Babe the sheep pig snuggled down in his bed of straw, closed his eyes, and fell sound asleep.